FRIENDS
Again

Under the direction of Romain Lizé, CEO, Magnificat
Editor, Magnificat: Isabelle Galmiche
Editor, Ignatius: Vivian Dudro
Translator: Janet Chevrier
Proofreader: Kathleen Hollenbeck
Assistant to the Editor: Pascale van de Walle
Layout Designers: Thérèse Jauze, Gauthier Delauné
Production: Thierry Dubus, Sabine Marioni

Original French edition: *Comme c'est doux de faire la paix*
© 2019 by Mame, Paris.
© 2019 by Magnificat, New York • Ignatius Press, San Francisco
All rights reserved.
ISBN Ignatius Press 978-1-62164-338-8 • ISBN Magnificat 978-1-949239-23-2
The trademark Magnificat depicted in this publication is used under license from
and is the exclusive proper ty of Magnificat Central Service Team, Inc., A Ministry to
Catholic Women, and may not be used without its written consent.

✳ KARINE-MARIE AMIOT ✳ VIOLAINE COSTA ✳

FRIENDS
Again

MAGNIFICAT · Ignatius

Henry likes to build things.
He makes planes and cars and gadgets
out of scraps of wood, cardboard boxes,
and other items people
throw away.

Emma likes to read.
She also likes to write stories
of her own and draw pictures.

Lost in her own world, Emma is skipping
and running toward Henry's plane.
"Watch out!" shouts Henry.
"Don't break my flying machine!"

But Emma ignores her brother.
She trips and falls on top
of Henry's plane.

"Emma!" yells Henry.
He kicks the pieces of his broken plane
and shouts at her, "Look at what you've done."

Emma is upset at the sight,
and she feels sorry.

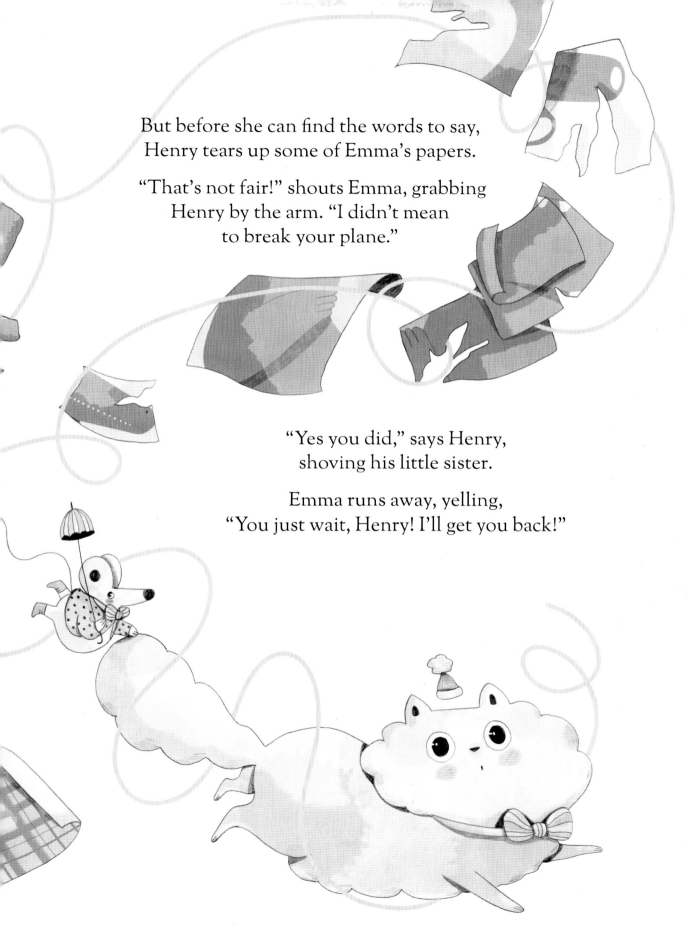

But before she can find the words to say,
Henry tears up some of Emma's papers.

"That's not fair!" shouts Emma, grabbing
Henry by the arm. "I didn't mean
to break your plane."

"Yes you did," says Henry,
shoving his little sister.

Emma runs away, yelling,
"You just wait, Henry! I'll get you back!"

Henry does not feel sorry for tearing up his sister's papers.

Emma no longer feels sorry
for breaking Henry's plane.

But in his heart, Henry feels a lump of sadness,
like a big knotted ball of string.

Emma feels one in her heart too.

After a while, Emma takes a few steps toward her brother
and Henry takes a few steps toward his sister.

Finally, they come face to face.
But neither of them is smiling.

"That was all your fault, Emma. You started it.
You broke my plane on purpose," says Henry.

"It was an accident," says Emma.
"But you tore up my drawings to get even!
That's much worse."

The knots grow tighter and heavier.

"That's it!" yells Henry. "I'll never play with you again!"

"I don't care," Emma shouts.

They each take an end of string and pull.

Heave-ho! It's a tug-of-war!

"I'm bigger and stronger than you are," says Henry.

"That doesn't make you better," says Emma.

Suddenly both children fall flat on their bottoms. Ouch!
But they feel more sad than hurt.

They feel very far away from each other.

The children have tummy aches from all these knots.
"I know I lost my temper," Henry thinks,
"but Emma should say sorry first."
"I know I should say sorry," Emma thinks,
"but Henry was so mean."

The children pace back
and forth in silence.

They both wish they could be
friends again.

Finally, they make up their minds.

At the same moment, they both say,
"I'm sorry."

Henry and Emma smile at each other. And in their hearts
the knots gently begin to unravel.

Emma lays her head on her brother's shoulder and says,

"I hate it when we're angry with each other."

"Me, too," Henry replies.

Henry stretches and says,
"Time to fix my flying machine."

"Can I help?" asks Emma.
"If you promise to be really careful," says Henry.
"And you can come with me on my next flight.
We could fly far, far away."

Emma's eyes light up:
"Maybe all the way to the stars!"

Printed in Malaysia in December 2019 by Tien Wah Press.
Job number MGN 20001
Printed in compliance
with the Consumer Protection Safety Act, 2008

MIX
Paper from
responsible sources
FSC® C012700
FSC
www.fsc.org